# Bee and Bug at Croak Castle

# Beetle and Bug at Croak Castle

Illustrated by Sonia Holleyman

Written by Hiawyn Oram

ORCHARD BOOKS

ORCHARD BOOKS
96 Leonard Street, London EC2A 4RH
*Orchard Books Australia*
14 Mars Road, Lane Cove, NSW 2066
ISBN 1 85213 889 0 (hardback)
ISBN 1 86039 008 0 (paperback)
First published in Great Britain 1995
First paperback publication 1996
Text © Hiawyn Oram 1995
Illustrations © Sonia Holleyman 1995
A CIP catalogue record for this book is available from the
British Library.
Printed in Great Britain by Guernsey Press, C.I.

The postman was early, he'd been
    and he'd gone,
With a letter for Bug from his great-
    uncle John.

'Come for the weekend,' was
scrawled on its pages,
'Aint seen you and Beetle for ages
and ages'.

"T'would be rude to refuse," said
  Beetle to Bug,
"And it won't take us long on our
  magical rug.
And besides, the old boy has such
  a bad cough
That any day now he might simply
  pop off."

"You are right, you are right," said
Bug with a sigh,
"I'd be terribly sad if he did go and
die.
Though it's hardly surprising the
old boy's a wheezer,
His castle's a nightmare – it's cold
as a freezer."

So they packed lots of woollies

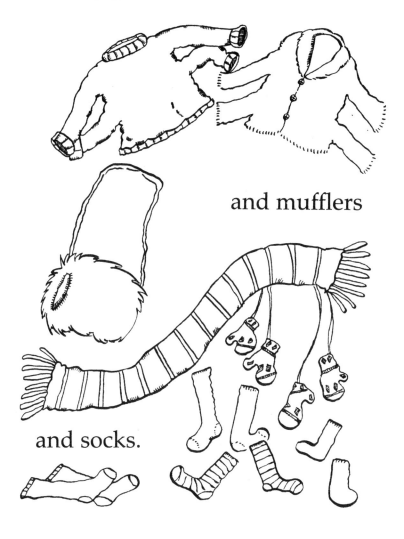

and mufflers

and socks.

And put out the garbage

and wound up the clocks.

And giving directions to Rug, left
   and right,
They arrived at Croak Castle by
   later that night.

"Uncle John, Uncle John?" Bug
called, as they landed –
the drawbridge was up and it
seemed they were stranded.

But the portcullis rose and down
    came the bridge.
A figure moved forward, a stranger
– a midge.

"Ah, Bug, my dear boy, and Beetle, how nice,
You remember your auntie – that's me – we've met twice.
Though I'm sorry to tell you your uncle's much worse,
Which is why I am here – I'm a fully trained nurse."

Then she bustled them into the
castle's great hall,
Where portraits of ancestors
lined every wall.

And offered them tea, which
they felt they should take
In spite of the fungus that
covered the cake.

But when they requested to see
  Uncle John,
Midge turned very ugly and
  choked on her scone.

"Your uncle's too sick to be seen
  or come down
And that's doctor's orders," she
  snapped with a frown.

And snatching a candle, she
 showed them the way
To the top of the castle, where they
 were to stay.

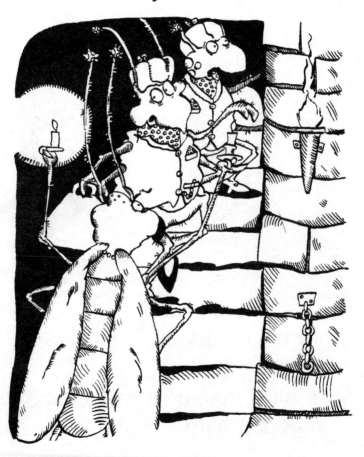

And when Bug suggested they'd
   need a small lamp,
As the room was so dark and the
   walls were so damp,

She nearly exploded, she swelled
with such hate,
They didn't dare ask for some coal
   for the grate.

"In this castle," she croaked, "*not* seeing is best.
*That* way you might get a decent night's rest."

"Oh, Beetle," said Bug, when
Midge closed the door,
"There's something quite wrong
here, I know it, I'm sure.

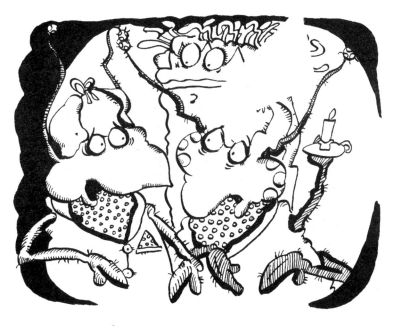

I don't have an aunt – not like
her – I detect
She's an evil impostor – the
worst, I suspect."

"Then let's get some sleep, "
    said Beetle, "tonight,
And deal with the problem
    tomorrow, all right?"
But as soon as they'd got
    themselves settled in bed . . .

Came a tap at the window that
filled them with dread.

"Oh, no! It's the Deathwatch –
    that hag of the dribble!"
Squawked Beetle to Bug, and
    Bug didn't quibble,

But pulled up the bedcovers
    over his nose
As his heart nearly stopped and
    his blood nearly froze.

"The Deathwatch, that Banshee of
    Bugs with her tapping,
Is an omen, a sign, and we can't be
    caught napping.

My uncle's in danger," said Bug,
   "There's no doubt
For Banshees appear when there's
   murder about!"

So quaking and quivering, they
    quickly re-dressed,
And crept from their room on
    their dangerous quest
To uncover the truth and save
    Uncle John
From the fake Auntie Midge and
    the strange goings-on.

"Oh, Beetle!" said Bug, as they
   came down the stair,
"This castle is haunted, I know
   by my hair,
Which is standing so straight it is
   piercing my hat,

And what is that drumming?
And wait . . . look at that!"

And now as they entered the
   castle's great hall,
With the ancestors watching it all
from the wall,

A ghost of a bug in an old army coat
Was beating a drum on one
     ghostly note.

"Take a breath, count to ten,"
  whispered Bug, "and swallow,
For it seems he is trying to get us
  to follow."

"Well, we can't," answered
   Beetle, "we're not made of air,
And he's just disappeared through
   that wall over there . . ."

"Well, it's prob'ly a sign," said
    Bug, "of a door
To some secret passage and some
    secret floor
And prob'ly he's tempting us,
    luring us on . . ."

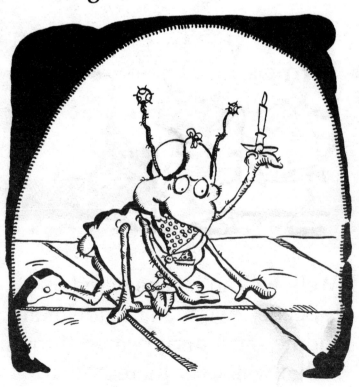

"Or trying to lead us," said
Beetle, "to John!"

And before they could properly
search for the door
In the blocks of blank stone, or
the flags of the floor,

A panicky sound, a scurrying,
was heard . . .

And there was the ghost of a
ladybird.

She was carrying a lamp and she
    flitted so fast,
She was here, she was gone, and
    Bug was aghast,

"Now that's a good ghost, we must
    follow her,
I'll do it alone if you really prefer . . ."

39

But Beetle was not giving up on
   his friend.
"I'll go with you, Bug, to the
   last, to the end."
So keeping to shadows, they
   followed the lamp

Down
hundreds
of steps
till they
came to
a ramp.

41

And there the ghost turned with a
  look that said, *Wait,*
*Tread carefully now and don't seal
  your fate.*

Then vanished and left them to
face what they'd found,
Which was Midge in a kitchen
deep underground.

She was cutting

and chopping

and stirring a stew,

Which was clearly a horribly
poisonous brew.

She was laughing and talking
while throwing in wine,
"With this to disguise it, they'll
think it tastes fine."

Bug motioned to Beetle, "We're best
    out of here
Before we are mincemeat or froth
    on her beer."

Then they scuttled and scrambled
and ran for their room,

Where dawn was just breaking and
lifting the gloom.

"She's got Uncle John! I knew it,
    I knew,"
Said Bug, "and she's feeding him
    poisonous stew.

And there's no time to lose, no time
    to discuss,
For now she is planning on
    poisoning us!"

So taking their rug from the
    hearth with no fire,
They made for the ramparts and
    boarded their flier.

And flew round the castle to snoop
 and to peer
Through each of the windows, the
 front and the rear.

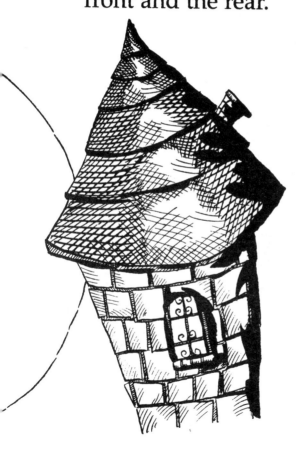

Till at last, as they hoped, through
   a grimy glass pane
They saw Uncle John, in distress,
   it was plain.

He was gagged, he was bound to
a chair, he was trapped,

"He can't get to the window,"
Bug cried as he rapped.

And then, to their total
    amazement they saw
The ghost drummer bug sort of . . .

drift through the door.

And out from the bed drapes the
ladybird merged,

"NOW OPEN THE WINDOW, "
Bug desperately urged.

Then together those ghosts
    somehow loosened the catch,
And pushing and pulling, they
    lifted the latch.

And Beetle and Bug, with their rug
    looking on,
Climbed into the room and untied
    Uncle John.

Then helping him squeeze through
the window to Rug,
Who took off at once without
orders from Bug.

They went like the wind – and it's
one of Rug's boasts
That on board, with the others, that
day, were two ghosts.

As for Midge, John's half-brother,
   disguised as the nurse,
Who was after John's castle, his
   land and his purse,

When he found they'd escaped,
   had a fit and fell out
Of an upper floor window. . .

and was lunch for a trout.

While Great-Uncle John settled
    down for a visit
At Beetle and Bug's, where he
    said, "It's exquisite!
I am warm, I am cosy, I am
    cooked Sunday roasts,
By my favourite young nephew

– plus Beetle and ghosts."